Hi, I'm Emily Elizabeth.
My dog, Clifford, and I love Christmas.
I remember the very first Christmas
Clifford spent with us.

He was a really tiny puppy back then.
He had never seen a Christmas tree before.

NORMAN BRIDWELL
Clifford's
FIRST CHRISTMAS

On Christmas Eve, we got out the decorations.

I held down a branch so Clifford could hang
a candy cane on it.

My hand slipped!

Clifford didn't like it at the
top of the tree.
Daddy had to rescue him.

The tree looked beautiful.

Clifford found a ball to play with.
He swung at the big ornament...

...but it swung right back.
Poor little puppy.

Next, I wrapped some gifts.

Clifford helped.

At last it was time for bed.
I tucked Clifford in.

Mom turned out the lights and said good-night.

Clifford couldn't sleep.
He went out to investigate.

Then somebody dropped in.

Santa was about to fill my stocking....

What a surprise!

Santa told us we had to go to sleep so that he could deliver our presents.

In the morning, we found he had left a little gift for Clifford.

And there were lots of gifts for the rest of us, too.

Clifford got other nice toys, too,
but he liked mine better.

He pretended to be a giant dog in my dollhouse...

...and a tunnel for my miniature train.

He played horse for my Thumbelina doll. Imagine a dog big enough to ride. What a silly idea, I thought.

Even though Clifford is big now,
he's still my very special Christmas puppy.